Sigmund Brouwer

Watch Out for Joel!

Strunk Soup

BETHANY
BACKYARD®
www.bethanyhouse.com

Strunk Soup
Copyright © 2003
Sigmund Brouwer

Cover and interior illustrations by Tammie Lyon/Laurie Lambert Association
Cover design by Jennifer Parker

Unless otherwise identified, Scripture quotations are from the *International Children's Bible,
New Century Version,* copyright © 1986, 1988 by Word Publishing, Dallas, Texas 75039. Used by
permission.

Published by Bethany House Publishers
11400 Hampshire Avenue South
Bloomington, Minnesota 55438

Bethany House Publishers is a division of
Baker Publishing Group, Grand Rapids, Michigan.

Printed in China

Library of Congress Cataloging-in-Publication Data

Brouwer, Sigmund, 1959-
   Strunk soup / by Sigmund Brouwer.
     p. cm. — (Watch out for Joel!)
Summary: Ricky and Joel are not sure how to tell Mrs. Strunk, their neighbor, that they do not
want to eat the supper she has prepared for them.
   ISBN 0-7642-2585-5 (pbk. : alk. paper)
   [1. Etiquette—Fiction. 2. Kindness—Fiction. 3. Brothers—Fiction. 4. Christian life—Fiction.]
I. Title. II. Series: Brouwer, Sigmund, 1959-   . Watch out for Joel!

   PZ7.B79984St   2003
   [E]—dc21

2003013804

Caring and Sharing

When Ricky and Joel are at Mrs. Strunk's house, she makes them supper. Will they be able to eat it?

Mark 4:24 says, "The way you give to others is the way God will give to you. But God will give you more than you give." Ricky and Joel are kind and caring to Mrs. Strunk. As you read the story, can you think of a time when you were kind like Joel and Ricky were?

1

It was suppertime. Joel sat at the kitchen table in Mrs. Strunk's house. He was seven.

Ricky sat at the kitchen table, too. He was Joel's brother. Ricky was thirteen.

Mrs. Strunk stood in the kitchen in front of her stove.

Mrs. Strunk was a neighbor to Joel and Ricky. Mrs. Strunk was a nice old lady.

But Mrs. Strunk was a very bad cook.

"I am so glad your mother and father decided to go to a movie tonight," Mrs. Strunk said to Joel and Ricky. "I am so glad your mother and father brought you here tonight to let me cook for you."

Joel was not glad. Ricky was not glad. The food on the stove smelled bad.

"Yes," Mrs. Strunk said. "I want to make sure that you have healthy food."

The food on the stove did not smell healthy.

"Yes," Mrs. Strunk said. "I am making onion soup. Stewed beets. And fried liver. I hope you like it."

Joel did not answer. He did not want to hurt Mrs. Strunk's feelings.

Ricky did not answer. He did not want to hurt Mrs. Strunk's feelings.

Mrs. Strunk was a nice old lady. But Mrs. Strunk was a very bad cook.

"Will you eat everything?" she asked Joel and Ricky.

"Yes," Joel finally said. He did not want to hurt Mrs. Strunk's feelings.

"Yes," Ricky finally said. He did not want

to hurt Mrs. Strunk's feelings.

"Good," Mrs. Strunk said. "It is nearly ready for you to eat. Onion soup and stewed beets and fried liver."

2

Mrs. Strunk was a nice old lady.

But Mrs. Strunk was a very bad cook.

Mrs. Strunk began to shake a can of pepper. She began to shake the pepper into the pot of onion soup.

Mrs. Strunk shook too much pepper out of the can. She shook the can of pepper too hard.

Some of the pepper floated into the air.

Some of the pepper floated up to Mrs. Strunk's nose.

Mrs. Strunk breathed in some of the pepper.

Mrs. Strunk sneezed.

Mrs. Strunk sneezed into the pot of onion soup.

Joel saw Mrs. Strunk sneeze into the pot of onion soup.

Ricky saw Mrs. Strunk sneeze into the pot of onion soup.

Mrs. Strunk was a nice old lady.

But Mrs. Strunk was a very bad cook.

"The soup is nearly ready," she said to Ricky and Joel. "I hope you eat all of it."

Joel did not want to eat the onion soup.

Ricky did not want to eat the onion soup.

But Mrs. Strunk was a nice old lady. Joel did not want to hurt her feelings. Ricky did not want to hurt her feelings.

So they did not answer. They did not want to eat the soup. Not after Mrs. Strunk sneezed in it.

3

Mrs. Strunk was a nice old lady.

But Mrs. Strunk was a very bad cook.

Mrs. Strunk shook the can of pepper again. She shook the pepper into the stewed beets.

Mrs. Strunk shook too much pepper out of the can. She shook the can of pepper too hard.

Some of the pepper floated into the air. Some of the pepper floated up to Mrs. Strunk's nose.

Mrs. Strunk breathed in some of the pepper.

Mrs. Strunk sneezed.

This time, she sneezed into the stewed beets.

Joel saw Mrs. Strunk sneeze into the stewed beets.

Ricky saw Mrs. Strunk sneeze into the stewed beets.

Mrs. Strunk was a nice old lady.

But Mrs. Strunk was a very bad cook.

"The stewed beets are nearly ready," she said to Ricky and Joel. "I hope you eat all of them."

Joel did not want to eat the stewed beets.

Ricky did not want to eat the stewed beets.

But Mrs. Strunk was a nice old lady. Joel did not want to hurt her feelings. Ricky did not want to hurt her feelings.

So they did not answer.

But they did not want to eat the stewed beets. Not after Mrs. Strunk sneezed in them.

4

Mrs. Strunk began to shake a can of pepper again. She began to shake the pepper into the fried liver.

Mrs. Strunk shook too much pepper out of the can. She shook the can of pepper too hard.

Some of the pepper floated into the air.

Some of the pepper floated up to Mrs. Strunk's nose.

Mrs. Strunk breathed in some of the pepper.

Mrs. Strunk sneezed.

This time, Mrs. Strunk sneezed so hard that her hands flew straight up into the air.

She was still holding the can of pepper.

When her hands flew straight up into the air, she threw a whole bunch of pepper dust into the air, too.

Mrs. Strunk threw all of the pepper straight into her face.

She breathed all of the pepper.

It made her sneeze again.

And again.

And again.

Mrs. Strunk went into a sneezing fit.

She sneezed so hard and so long that her wig twisted loose.

Mrs. Strunk was a nice old lady.

But Mrs. Strunk was a very bad cook.

She sneezed so hard that the wig fell off her head.

5

Where did Mrs. Strunk's wig land?

Not in the onion soup.

Not in the pot of beets.

Not in the pan with fried liver.

No.

Mrs. Strunk's wig landed on one of the burners of the stove.

Joel did not know what to say.

Ricky did not know what to say.

Mrs. Strunk did not know what to say.

Mrs. Strunk quickly grabbed the wig. She grabbed it from the burner of the stove. She put it back on her head.

"There," she said to Joel and Ricky. "Let us pretend that did not happen. Let us pretend you did not see it."

"Yes," Joel said.

"Yes," Ricky said.

Mrs. Strunk was a nice old lady.

But Mrs. Strunk was a very bad cook.

"Are you ready for the onion soup?" she asked Joel and Ricky. "Are you ready for stewed beets and fried liver?"

Joel did not answer. He pointed at Mrs. Strunk's head.

Ricky did not answer. He pointed at Mrs. Strunk's head.

Mrs. Strunk's wig had landed on the burner of the stove. Mrs. Strunk had put her wig on very quickly.

Now flames came out of the back of Mrs. Strunk's wig.

6

"Mrs. Strunk!" Joel shouted.

"Mrs. Strunk!" Ricky shouted.

Right then, Mrs. Strunk felt that her wig was growing hot. It was growing too hot.

"Your wig is on fire!" Joel shouted.

"Your wig is on fire!" Ricky shouted.

"My wig is on fire!" Mrs. Strunk shouted.

Mrs. Strunk reached up.

Mrs. Strunk quickly threw her wig off her head.

Where did Mrs. Strunk's burning wig land?

Not in the onion soup.

Not in the pot of beets.

Not in the pan with fried liver.

Not on the burner of the stove.

Mrs. Strunk's burning wig landed near the window beside the stove.

The window had a curtain. Mrs. Strunk's burning wig landed under the curtain near the window beside the stove.

Mrs. Strunk was a nice old lady.

But Mrs. Strunk was a very bad cook.

Mrs. Strunk's burning wig touched the curtain near the window beside the stove.

7

The curtain near the window near the stove caught on fire.

"Mrs. Strunk!" Joel shouted.

"Mrs. Strunk!" Ricky shouted.

"Your curtain is on fire!" Joel shouted.

"Your curtain is on fire!" Ricky shouted.

"My curtain is on fire!" Mrs. Strunk shouted.

Joel ran for the fire extinguisher. Joel took it from the wall near the stove. Joel gave it to his older brother, Ricky.

Ricky knew what to do.

Ricky pulled the pin of the fire extinguisher. Ricky aimed the nozzle.

Ricky pulled the trigger.

Ricky shot white stuff out of the fire extinguisher.

Ricky covered the curtain with the white stuff. Ricky covered the wig with the white stuff. Ricky covered the stove with the white stuff.

And the fire was out.

8

Mrs. Strunk was a nice old lady.

But Mrs. Strunk was a very bad cook.

All of the onion soup was covered with white stuff from the fire extinguisher.

All of the pot of stewed beets was covered with white stuff.

All of the pan of fried liver was covered with white stuff.

Mrs. Strunk looked at the mess.

Joel looked at the mess.

Ricky looked at the mess.

"Well," Mrs. Strunk said to Joel and Ricky.

"You must still be hungry. You are growing boys. You need to eat."

Joel did not want to hurt Mrs. Strunk's feelings.

Ricky did not want to hurt Mrs. Strunk's feelings.

Mrs. Strunk was a nice old lady.

But Mrs. Strunk was a very bad cook.

Joel could not eat onion soup and stewed beets and fried liver covered with white stuff from a fire extinguisher.

Ricky could not eat onion soup and stewed beets and fried liver covered with white stuff from a fire extinguisher.

9

"Please," Joel said. "Don't ask us to eat that."

"Please," Ricky said. "Don't ask us to eat that."

Mrs. Strunk laughed.

"The onion soup and stewed beets and fried liver are covered with white stuff from a fire extinguisher," Mrs. Strunk said. "I would not ask you to eat that."

"Oh," Joel said.

"Oh," Ricky said.

"First, we need to clean up this mess," Mrs.

Strunk said. "Then we will go out and get some pizza. Does that sound like a good idea?"

"Yes!" Joel said.

"Yes!" Ricky said.

Mrs. Strunk was a nice old lady.

But she was a very bad cook.

A Lesson About Caring

In *Strunk Soup*, Ricky and Joel try to be nice to Mrs. Strunk, but it isn't easy. Mrs. Strunk is a very bad cook!

It is important to be kind to others. This makes people happy, and it makes God happy, too. When Joel and Ricky were kind to Mrs. Strunk, it made her happy, and made them feel good. You can make others feel good by being kind to them.

To Talk About

1. How do you feel when others are kind to you?
2. Who can you think of that you can be kind to today?
3. What can you do to show God's love to others?

"To your service for God, add kindness for brothers and sisters in Christ, and to this kindness, add love."
2 Peter 1:7

Award-winning author Sigmund Brouwer inspires kids to love reading. From WATCH OUT FOR JOEL! to the ACCIDENTAL DETECTIVES series (full of stories about Joel's older brother, Ricky), Sigmund writes books that kids want to read again and again. Not only does he write cool books, Sigmund also holds writing camps and classes for more than ten thousand children each year!

You can read more about Sigmund, his books, and the Young Writer's Institute on his Web site, *www.coolreading.com*.